Charles Dickens

A Christmas Carol

Retold by Joshua George

Illustrated by Jennifer Miles

Loved by Kids
Tide Mill Way, Woodbridge, Suffolk, IP12 1AP, UK
Copyright © 2018 Imagine That Group Ltd
All rights reserved
0 2 4 6 8 9 7 5 3 1
Manufactured in China

ISBN 978-1-78700-885-4

A catalogue record for this book is available from the British Library

Scrooge was hard and sharp as flint!
The cold within him froze his old features,
and made his eyes red, and his thin lips blue.
He was a squeezing, wrenching, grasping,
scraping, clutching, and miserly man!

Scrooge's business partner, Jacob Marley,
had been dead seven years, but the
sign over the office door still said
'Scrooge and Marley.'

It was Christmas Eve and Scrooge was busy at work.

Across the room, Bob Cratchit tried to warm
himself at his candle. Scrooge was too
mean to put more coal on the fire.

'Merry Christmas, Uncle!'
cried a cheerful voice.
'I am collecting money for the poor.'
It was Scrooge's nephew, Fred.

'Bah!' said Scrooge. 'Humbug!'

'At least come for dinner with us tomorrow,' said Fred.

'Bah!' said Scrooge again. 'Humbug!'

At last it was time to close the office.
Bob Cratchit hurried home, but not before
stopping to slide down an icy hill.
It was Christmas Eve after all!

Christmas Eve was the same as any other day to Scrooge. His house was dark and dreary. Darkness was cheap, and Scrooge liked it.

As Scrooge sat alone he heard a strange noise, like someone dragging heavy chains up the stairs from the cellar.

'Humbug,' said Scrooge. 'I don't believe it.'

But Scrooge's face changed colour when a familiar figure appeared!

'I am the ghost of Jacob Marley,' cried the figure,
clanking the chains it dragged behind it.
'You will be haunted by three ghosts, Scrooge!
The first when the clock strikes one …'

Later that night, Scrooge awoke
to the 'Dong!' of the church bell!
Suddenly, the room filled with
light and Scrooge found
himself face to face with
a strange figure.

'Who are you?'
asked Scrooge.

'I am the Ghost of
Christmas Past,'
said the figure.
'Follow me.'

The ghost showed Scrooge many Christmases from his past …

I was a boy here!

It showed him the Christmas when Scrooge was left to spend the holidays at school, all alone.

It showed him a Christmas party given by his first boss, Mr Fezziwig.

Old Fezziwig made us all so happy!

Finally, the ghost showed Scrooge the Christmas he left Belle, his one true love, to concentrate on making money.

Show me no more!

'Dong!' Scrooge woke in his bed again.
When he opened the door to the next
room, green leaves decorated the walls,
and the loveliest Christmas foods were
heaped on the floor.

In the middle of the food sat a jolly giant.
'Come in!' boomed the giant.
'I am the Ghost of Christmas Present!'

The second ghost showed Scrooge many different Christmases ...

First it took him to Bob Cratchit's house. Although the Cratchits were poor, their little house was filled with happiness. 'God bless us, every one,' said the sickly-looking Tiny Tim.

Will Tiny Tim live?

Then the ghost took Scrooge to his nephew Fred's house. It was full of Christmas fun and laughter.

In every house they visited the ghost sprinkled the spirit of Christmas.

'Dong!' The church bell struck again and the Ghost of Christmas Present disappeared. In its place stood a tall, mysterious ghost, wrapped in a black cloak. 'Are you the Ghost of Christmas Yet to Come?' asked Scrooge. The ghost said nothing, but just pointed forward. 'Lead on!' said Scrooge. 'I will follow you. Lead on, Ghost!'

The third ghost showed Scrooge Christmases that had not yet happened ...

It showed him people talking about a man who had died. The man had been so mean that no one missed him.

My life is like his.

It showed him Bob Cratchit's house.
Before it had been full of noise,
but now it was quiet and Tiny
Tim's little chair stood empty.

Poor Tiny Tim!

Finally the ghost took Scrooge to a
churchyard and pointed to a grave.
Scrooge crept, trembling, towards
it and read his own name.

EBENEZER
SCROOGE

*I can change,
I promise!*

Scrooge woke and
ran to the window.
'What day is it?'
he called to a
boy outside.

'Why, Christmas Day!'
replied the boy.

'Ha!' laughed Scrooge.
'I haven't missed it!
Merry Christmas everybody!'

Scrooge gave the boy money to buy the biggest turkey in the shop. 'I'll send it to Bob Cratchit's,' he laughed. 'It's twice the size of Tiny Tim!'

That afternoon, Scrooge went to dinner at his nephew's house. He was the perfect guest and joined in all the fun. And what's more, he gave a very large donation to the poor.

The next morning, Scrooge was at work extra early.

'You're late!' he growled, when Bob Cratchit arrived.
'I am not going to stand for this any longer … I am going to raise your pay, and try to help you and your family, Bob!'

Scrooge was better than his word. He did it all, and much more, and to Tiny Tim, who did NOT die, he was a second father.

And so, as Tiny Tim said, 'God bless us, every one!'